Melissa Di Donato Roos was born in New York and at a young age knew she wanted to make a mark on the world. Melissa was determined to have a positive impact on building confidence and bravery in young girls, so that the world would be full of determined and independent women. She entered the field of technology at the start of her career and has always been committed to ensuring a diverse and inclusive workplace. She is the first female CEO of SUSE, one of the world's largest Open Source technology companies.

As a thought leader and passionate supporter of women in technology, Melissa has received several industry awards and is recognised as one of the most transformative CEOs in the tech industry.

Melissa, with her husband, is the co-founder of Inner Wings, a charitable foundation dedicated to empowering young girls to be brave and confident. All the proceeds from *Kick Like a Girl*, along with Melissa's two other children's books *How Do Mermaids Poo?* and *The Magic Box* are invested into Inner Wings to fund confidence-building programmes for girls around the world.

Melissa Di Donato Roos

Kick like a girl

Illustrated by ange allen

AUSTIN MACAULEY PUBLISHERS™
LONDON • CAMBRIDGE • NEW YORK • SHARJAH

A CIP catalogue record for this title is available from the British Library.

ISBN 9781398423350 (Paperback)
ISBN 9781398423367 (Hardback)
ISBN 9781398423374 (ePub e-book)

www.austinmacauley.com

First Published (2021)
Austin Macauley Publishers Ltd
25 Canada Square
Canary Wharf
London
E14 5LQ

This book is dedicated to my husband, DR, for having more belief in me than I do in myself. Without you, this book would never exist. Thank you for aiming for the stars while holding my hand and making my dreams come true.

To my confident and passionate daughter, FDR, who is the sunshine in my everyday life. You inspire me in so many ways to always be my best.

Finally, to all the lovely girls in our world like MFG, LFG, MD, OD, LT, all the Y3ND girls, and so many more.

You are driven, clever and brave. You will, one day, RULE THE WORLD!

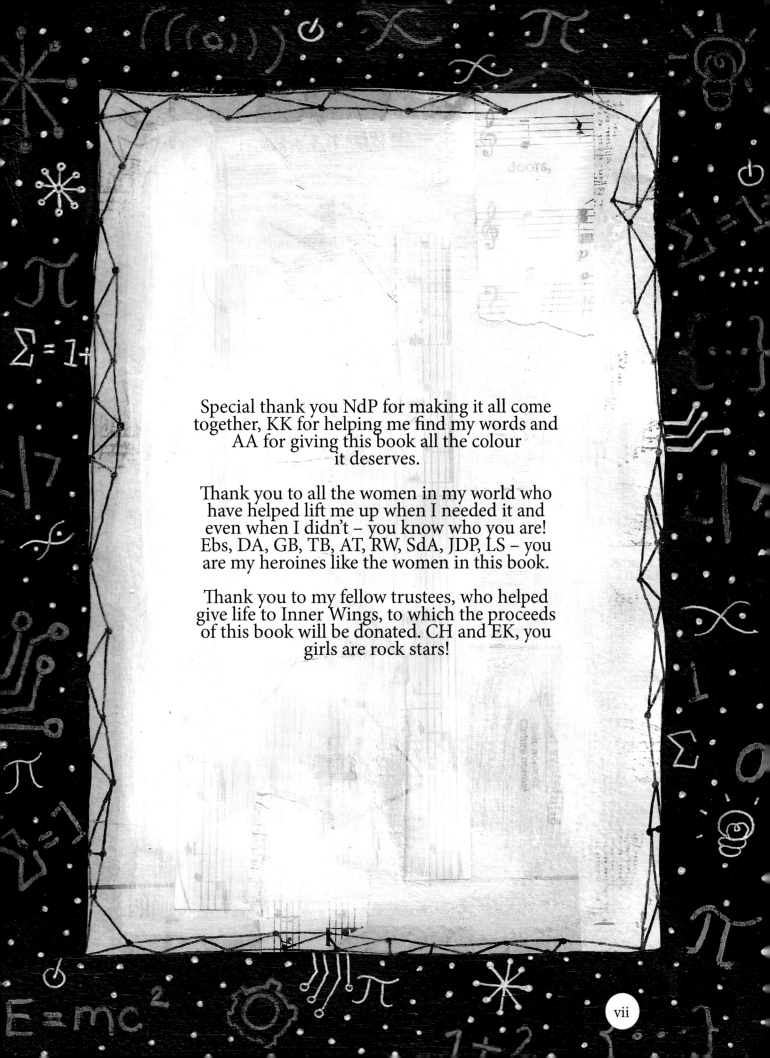

Special thank you NdP for making it all come together, KK for helping me find my words and AA for giving this book all the colour it deserves.

Thank you to all the women in my world who have helped lift me up when I needed it and even when I didn't – you know who you are! Ebs, DA, GB, TB, AT, RW, SdA, JDP, LS – you are my heroines like the women in this book.

Thank you to my fellow trustees, who helped give life to Inner Wings, to which the proceeds of this book will be donated. CH and EK, you girls are rock stars!

Francesca skipped along happily,
Nala at her side.
Singing as she went,
and smiling oh so wide!

They reached the park on Carefree Lane,
all her friends were having fun.
On swings, on slides and see-saws,
the day had just begun.

10610–17

Francesca heard a "THWACK!"
and then a raucous cheer.
She wondered what was happening,
when a grubby boy came near.

"Have you seen my ball?" he asked,
"It must have come this way.
Our game is only halfway done,
I need to get back right away."

Francesca helped him look
and found the missing ball.
She dug it out from a thorny bush
and gave the boy a call.

"Here you go," Francesca said,
passing the football back.
"If you're playing a game,
I'm really good at offensive attack!"

"Play with us?!" the boy exclaimed,
his surprise he could not hide.
"You can watch," he said at once,
"Girls can't kick a football!" he emphasised.

"It's only a game" Francesca tried,
"I've played lots of times before.
I'm good at defending
and I know just how to score."

12

"Girls cannot play football!" the boy laughed,
as he cleaned the ball on his shirt.
"Girls are meant to do ballet,
not roll around in the dirt."

"You KICK LIKE A GIRL,
and we want to win.
Our team has to be strong,
we can't let girls in!"

Off he ran to play his game,
leaving Francesca alone.
She hung her head and with her dog,
she turned to go back home.

"I don't feel much like playing today,"
she whispered down to Nala.
They plodded back along Dreary Lane,
Francesca feeling somewhat smaller.

She entered the house slowly,
through the kitchen door.
Bewildered, angry and sad,
she plopped down on the floor.

"What's going on?" asked her Mum,
"you seem so upset today."
"Oh Mamma..." Francesca began to cry,
"The boys wouldn't let me play."

"I just wanted to join the football match,
is that too much to ask?!
They said I 'kick like a girl' and that
this would guarantee them placing last."

"I guess I'll just go
and give my friend Ila a call.
She always says yes,
when I ask her to play ball."

"Hang on just a moment, Franche,"
Mum said lovingly.
She wrapped her arms around her tight
"Come sit here, on my knee."

"Now listen closely, this is important...
it's not just a game of ball.
I don't want anyone to dull your sparkle
or make you feel so small."

"You're as fast as lightening,
and you have a powerful shot.
What the boys don't realise is
your mind is the strongest thing you've got."

"So here's the deal... let's talk it through,
then, I want you to go back.
Just hear what I have to say
and cut yourself some slack."

"Girls can do anything,
if they want it badly enough.
Some people say we're weaker
but we're actually very tough."

19

"Once upon a time...
there was a girl named Frida Kahlo.
A road accident left her crippled
and as a child she suffered from Polio."

"Her life was full of pain,
she might have chosen to quit.
Instead she took up painting to pass the
time and the world fell in love with it."

"Her artwork was so unique,
it showed an honest heart.
Unapologetic about who she was,
iconic unibrow from the start."

"Frida painted to free her mind
and as the years went by, she said,
'Feet, what do I need you for
when I have wings to fly instead!'"

"Not only was she a painter," said Mum,
"she gave hope to an entire nation."
"Wow!" Francesca softly said,
"She was quite an inspiration."

"And there's an American politician,
Madeleine Albright, she is great!
Ambassador to the United Nations,
the first female secretary of State."

"A forceful champion of democracy,
she has battled some amazing fights.
Her strong beliefs supported other women,
and protected human rights."

"A professor and an author too,
so many powerful roles to hold.
An example to us girls,
to be just as brave and bold."

"Have you heard of Ada Lovelace?"
Mum had a twinkle in her eye.
"Who was she, Mum?" Francesca asked,
her eyes beginning to dry.

"Ada was born to a father
who rather wanted a son.
Her mother sometimes called her 'It',
little Ada must have felt shunned."

"She was bright as a button
and began to really excel.
Especially in Maths and Science,
she performed particularly well."

"She used poetic, creative thought
to figure out maths problems.
Whatever sums she was given,
she somehow managed to solve them."

"She worked alongside Babbage,
the father of modern computers.
Ada became the very first programmer,
the pride of all her tutors."

"She wrote an algorithm
to use technology as a tool.
Because of her, we can use
computers at home and at school."

"Plagued with illness, and with three
children for whom to care,
Ada Lovelace is a hero
for women and men, everywhere."

Francesca took a moment
and began to think out loud.
"I guess I should be sure, like them,
I should be brave and be proud."

"Yes, my Franche, that you should.
These women fought for so long,
so that we wouldn't have the same battles,
they are an inspiration to be strong."

"You already have a loving heart
and a beautiful, intelligent mind.
We must also remember
to be strong, humble and to be kind."

"Be just like Rosa Parks,
the First Lady of civil rights.
She was arrested for speaking her mind,
so began a 381-day long fight."

"Rosa refused to give up her seat
to a white man on a bus.
'No, I won't.' she simply said.
It caused a great big fuss."

"'All I was doing was trying
to get home from work', she said.
But she did infinitely more than that.
She became a civil-rights figure-head."

"Then there's Amelia Earhart,
an aviation pioneer and an author.
She was the first female to fly across the Atlantic.
Remember... she was also someone's daughter."

"She set so many records,
in an industry of men.
Books about her adventures
were best sellers back then."

"She founded a group of female pilots,
they were called The 99s.
She was a couageous adventurer,
a role model who shines."

"Mamma, I want to be courageous,
like all the women here.
I also want to be honest,
I can't pretend to not feel fear."

Mum replied knowingly,
she knew just what Francesca meant.
"You'll learn to pitch courage in your heart,
just like a waterproof tent."

"Remind yourself daily that
you are courageous, strong, and smart.
Try time and time again
until it's imprinted on your heart."

"Be like Marie Curie,
who fought from year to year.
She's an icon of the scientific world,
a professor and true pioneer."

"First woman to win a Nobel prize
in two different fields.
Her research in radiography
was true genius revealed!"

"She discovered Polonium and Radium,
she was so curious and devoted.
She had incorruptible modesty,
Einstein once noted!"

"Not only did she develop
the theory of radioactivity, there's more.
She drove her equipment to the frontlines,
to support soldiers in the first World War."

"So many tenacious spirits
and stories of women so tough.
Should I carry on,
or have you had enough?"

Francesca laughed at her Mum's words
and just sat there for a minute.
"I think you should tell me more.
My mind has space left in it."

"Well... Valentina Tereshkova,
was the first woman in space.
She was a Russian textile worker
and yet she still won the space race."

"She orbited the earth
forty-eight times.
This is twelve times more
than all the previous astronauts... combined!"

"And Florence Nightingale,
'The Lady of the Lamp.'
She changed the face of nursing, forever
from within an army camp."

"Long before all of these heroines
was The Mighty Queen Elizabeth the first.
She led with her heart
and it was all completely unrehearsed."

"However, the one who really stands out
and it is no mystery,
is a young girl from Pakistan
who went down in history."

"Her name is Malala Yousafzai.
She won a Nobel Peace prize too.
Speaking out about education for girls,
it's a vision she's seeing through."

"Her vocal demands were loud
and came at a very high cost.
Gunmen boarded her school bus, shot her three
times, her life was nearly lost."

"She chose not to cower or hide
or give up on her dream.
This incident made her stronger...
in my heart, she is a queen."

"So, before you give up on football
follow your dream,
and stand up for every girl
who's been told that they can't join a team!"

"The next time someone says you 'kick like a girl'
you must feel strong and proud.
Say, 'THANK YOU yes I do!'
Shout it out and say it loud."

36

Francesca smiled the sweetest smile,
then she grinned from ear to ear.
"Mamma, I'll try to be brave
but I feel a bit of fear."

"Oh, Franche!" Mum sighed,
giving her another hug.
"Here's the big secret,
my sweet, little cuddle bug..."

"It is okay to be fearful
but don't give in, be strong.
For you will find your confidence,
I promise it won't take long."

Francesca thought about it,
then called Ila to talk it through.
They put on their football kits,
they knew just what to do.

Together, they marched along Power Street,
making their way to the park.
Francesca had a thought,
it entered like a spark.

"I dare you to play me!"
she challenged the boy from earlier that day.
She said "If you win, I'll shake your hand,
and we'll walk away."

"But if we score more goals than you,
we want to join the team."
She knew that if they had a shot,
the girls would reign supreme.

Guess what happened, then?!
It's true... the girls are on the team!
Nala is their mascot,
they never gave up their dream.

Francesca and Ila said to the boys,
"Yes, we are girls and there is nothing we cannot do!
We can kick the ball, score a goal,
for there is no problem we can't get through!"

The boys learned a lesson
and the girls did too.
They would remember all the strong women
whenever they felt blue.

Kick like a girl and be proud,
hold your head high with confidence.
To 'kick like a girl' forever will mean
strength, power and intelligence!

The End